75293
Good Things Come in Small Packages

Anne Mazer
AR B.L.: 3.5
Points: 2.0   MG

The AMAZING DAYS of ABBY HAYES®

Good Things Come in Small Packages

Read more books about me!

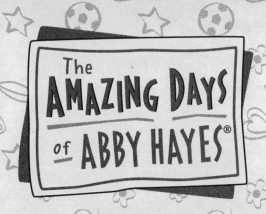

The AMAZING DAYS of ABBY HAYES®

Good Things Come in Small Packages

ANNE MAZER

AN
APPLE
PAPERBACK

SCHOLASTIC INC.
New York Toronto London Auckland Sydney
Mexico City New Delhi Hong Kong Buenos Aires

No part of this publication may be reproduced in whole or in part, or stored in a retrieval system, or transmitted in any form or by any means, electronic, mechanical, photocopying, recording, or otherwise, without written permission of the publisher. For information regarding permission, write to Scholastic Inc., Attention: Permissions Department, 557 Broadway, New York, NY 10012.

ISBN 0-439-48280-1

Illustrations by Monica Gesue

12 11 10 9 8 7 6   4 5 6 7 8/0

Printed in the U.S.A.   40

First printing, December 2003

For Marcia

Chapter 1

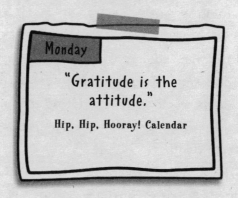

It <u>is</u>.

Okay. I will think of five things I am grateful for. That's <u>easy</u>!!!!

1. My new friend, Hannah.
2. Walking to school with Hannah.
3. Having Hannah in Ms. Kantor's fifth-grade class with me.
4. Coming home from school with Hannah.

Hannah is not the only person I am grateful for. I am also VERY grateful for . . .

5. Ms. Bunder and her weekly creative writing classes.

Our class missed creative writing last week because of Thanksgiving. I can't wait for this week's class. Ms. Bunder said we will split up into writers groups, just like real writers do!!!

Hooray!!! I hope that Hannah and I will be in the same writers group. Then I will be <u>extra</u> grateful!

"Why doesn't the sun come out?" Abby complained. "I'm sick of rain!"

Abby and Hannah walked slowly toward school. The sky was gray, and there was a light drizzle. It had been raining for days.

"I want snow!" Hannah cried. She wound a long striped scarf around her neck. "I *love* winter!"

"The best thing about winter is sitting inside with a book and a cup of hot chocolate," Abby said.

"That's fun," Hannah agreed. Her eyes sparkled. "But sledding, ice-skating, and skiing are fun, too."

"Yes, but I like summer so much better," said Abby.

"That's because your family goes camping," Hannah pointed out.

"You lived to tell the tale!" Abby joked.

Hannah had accompanied the Hayes family on a camping trip to the mountains the previous summer. She had survived bad weather, an overdose of blueberries, getting lost in the woods — and, of course, Abby's family.

"It was the best week of the summer," Hannah insisted.

She was cheerful about almost *everything*.

"You can say that now that it's over," Abby said.

Hannah stepped over a pile of slushy leaves. "Remember, my family moved this summer," she said. "I was packing and unpacking boxes for weeks."

"Ugh," Abby said.

"It was awful!" Hannah said. Then she brightened suddenly. "But now I live in your neighborhood. It's great here. And I like Ms. Kantor and Ms. Bunder and . . ."

"Hey, Hayes!" Casey hurried across the street to join the two girls.

"Hey, Hoffman!" Abby said, saluting Casey. It was their official greeting.

Casey was wearing a light jacket. His hair was wet from the rain. "Hi, Hannah!" he added.

"Hello," Hannah replied. "Just adding another *h* word," she explained.

"Hilarious," Casey answered.

"Help!" Abby cried. "Enough!"

Even though he was a boy, Casey was one of Abby's good friends. They had met when they worked together on a science project. Abby and Hannah were in Ms. Kantor's class. Casey was in the other fifth-grade class.

Abby, Hannah, and Casey walked in silence for a moment.

"So, what did you do over Thanksgiving?" Casey asked.

Hannah made a face. "We had relatives visiting from Ohio, New Hampshire, and Massachusetts. Three aunts, two uncles, seven cousins, and one grandfather."

"Was it fun?" Abby asked.

"There were three cousins sleeping in my room. One of them snored, one of them kicked my bed all night, and the other one kept getting up to go to the bathroom."

"That sounds like a nightmare," Casey commented.

"*Yes!*" Hannah agreed.

"You could have stayed at my house," Abby said to Hannah. "It was just us." Abby lived with her parents; older twin sisters, Eva and Isabel; and younger brother, Alex. "We had a quiet Thanksgiving. It was actually kind of boring."

"Maybe next year I'll sleep at your house," Hannah suggested, "and you can come to *our* house during the day. My cousins are great when they're awake."

"Let's ask our families if we can do that!" Abby cried.

Hannah smiled. "What did you do over the holidays, Casey?"

"We had the world's *worst* Thanksgiving meal ever!" Casey announced. "We were visiting my father's cousin George. He's a vegetarian. He served us beets, brussels sprouts, lentil stew, spelt bread, and unsweetened cranberry-apple pie with whole wheat crust."

"Ugh!!" Hannah and Abby said in unison.

"Yep," Casey agreed. "It was bad. After that

meal, my father said he'll never become a vegetarian."

"Bethany is a vegetarian," Hannah said, referring to one of their classmates. "I wonder if she eats like that."

"She had a normal Thanksgiving," Abby said. "Except for a tofu turkey."

"That sounds delicious compared to our Thanksgiving," Casey grumbled. "I wish my father's cousin George was *that* kind of vegetarian."

Abby, Hannah, and Casey walked past the fence that surrounded the elementary school and entered the playground.

"Another day of school," Abby sighed. "And three whole days before Ms. Bunder comes again. I can't wait until Thursday!"

"I love it here!" Hannah said. "Lancaster Elementary is so much better than my old school."

"Glad you like it," Casey said. "Our school *is* the best, isn't it?"

"Now you sound like Brianna," Abby teased.

Brianna was their classmate. She *always* liked to be number one.

"Brianna is nicer than some kids at my old

school," Hannah commented. "There were some really mean kids in my class."

"What about Victoria?" Casey asked, referring to Brianna's best friend. "She's in *my* class. I can't imagine anyone meaner than *she* is!"

"Like, yeah, you know, you're probably, like, right about that," Abby said, imitating Victoria's speech. "Too bad she's in your class. Lucky she's not in ours!"

The bell rang. Laughing, they hurried inside.

Chapter 2

Thursday

Good things come in small packages.

That's what Ms. Kantor told us yesterday. As a special project for the holidays, our class will make small packages of good things. We will send them to kids whose families can't afford presents. Ms. Kantor suggested that each of us fill a shoe box with inexpensive gifts, like small toys, games, puzzles, pencils, cards, socks, or mittens.

Next week, we'll each bring a shoe box to school and decorate it with colored paper. Then we'll fill the boxes with good things, and Ms. Kantor will deliver them.

Hooray! Lots of kids will have happier
holidays because of our small packages.
And our holidays will be happier, too.

A double <u>hooray</u>!!! Today is Thursday.
It is finally time for creative writing again.
I can't wait to see Ms. Bunder!

"Today is writers group day," Ms. Bunder announced.
"Have any of you ever been in a writers group?"

Everyone shook their head.

"I'll start from the beginning, then," Ms. Bunder
said with a smile.

Abby sighed with happiness. This was the best moment of the best day in the week. It was hard to believe that only a few years ago, Ms. Bunder had been
baby-sitting Ms. Kantor's kids. Now she was Abby's
favorite teacher *ever*. And she always had cool
clothes. Today she wore an orange sweater with a
beaded flower design and white pants.

"She looks like an ice-cream cone," Hannah whispered to Abby. "Orange sherbet and vanilla ice
cream."

"With sprinkles," Natalie added, pointing to the
beaded flowers.

Natalie's short dark hair was messy, as if she had just run her hands through it. She wore one turquoise sock and one pink sock. Her fingers had smears of paint and ink on them. Once she had been one of Abby's best friends. They were still good friends, but Natalie now spent a lot of time with Bethany.

"I love sprinkles!" Hannah exclaimed.

"Me, too," Natalie said.

"*Ssshh,*" Abby whispered. "I want to hear Ms. Bunder."

". . . divide into groups," Ms. Bunder was saying, "and listen to one another read."

Read what? Did writers groups involve reading? Weren't they supposed to be about *writing*?

Abby looked over at Mason. "Did you hear what she said?"

Mason didn't answer. He pretended to pick his nose.

"Thanks a lot," Abby said. She raised her hand. "Ms. Bunder? Could you repeat that?"

Ms. Bunder didn't get annoyed at Abby's question like some teachers would. She repeated the instructions calmly. "You're going to choose five words from a list and write a short story using them." She glanced at the clock. "In half an hour, you'll read your stories to one another in small groups." Ms. Bunder added, "And then you'll give feedback."

The fifth-graders looked at one another in alarm.

"Feedback?" Tyler said. "Isn't that something that happens with loudspeakers?"

"It's constructive criticism," Ms. Bunder explained. "Building up, not tearing down. You're going to help one another become better writers."

"What if someone's piece stinks?" Mason asked.

"Mine won't," Brianna announced. "Everyone will think mine is the best. *Oui, oui?*" she added in French.

" 'Weee, weee,' said the three little pigs," Natalie muttered.

"First of all, find something good to say about each person's writing," Ms. Bunder said. "If there's something you don't like, try to explain in a helpful way."

"Like instead of saying, 'That's terrible,' say, 'That's terrible because it's boring'?" Zach asked.

Ms. Bunder smiled. "How would you feel if I said that to you, Zach?"

"Oh, fine," Zach said.

Brianna's hand shot into the air. "You should say, 'Your piece is good, but you could put more excitement and action into it.' "

"Yes!" Ms. Bunder agreed.

"The way *I* do," Brianna concluded triumphantly.

"What about, 'I like the way you describe people, but you should have something happen in your story'?" Abby said.

"Great," Hannah whispered.

"Perfect!" Ms. Bunder said.

Abby blushed. Mason stuck out his tongue at her.

Brianna tossed her hair over her shoulder and sighed dramatically. "*My* explanation was more perfect."

Ms. Bunder picked up a stack of papers and began to pass them out. "I think you all understand what's expected. You're ready to be part of a real writers group."

" 'And so the marvelous and wonderful story of me is finished,' " Brianna read, " 'but only for today. Stay tuned for my brilliant, exciting future,' " she concluded with a flourish. She put down her paper and looked around the group expectantly.

"Um . . ." Abby began, then fell silent.

Natalie stared at the floor.

Bethany swung her foot back and forth.

Mason burped.

"Well?" Brianna demanded.

There was an uncomfortable silence.

"You have dramatic flair," Hannah said suddenly. "Your story has lots of drama in it."

Everyone in the group breathed a sigh of relief.

Brianna looked pleased. "My life *is* drama. I'm the lead in every play."

"Really?" Hannah said.

"Except when *I* am," Natalie corrected. She had competed against Brianna and won the lead role in the school play.

Brianna frowned at Natalie. "*That* was a tragic mistake," she said.

"Are there any other characters in your story?" Abby asked. "It seems like it's all about you."

"Of course it is," Brianna said.

"You ought to write about animals," Bethany said. "Like hamsters."

"I know that's what *you* wrote about," Brianna said scornfully.

Abby glanced at Natalie.

Once Bethany had been a Brianna clone. Her cheer of "Yay, Brianna!" had echoed through the halls of Lancaster Elementary. Now Bethany had declared her independence from Brianna.

"Hamsters are lovable and intelligent, especially Blondie." Bethany defended her beloved pet, even though no one had said anything against her.

"Oh, *really*?" Brianna said. "You believe that?"

Bethany's eyes narrowed. Her face turned red.

"You wrote about your hamster?" Hannah interjected. "I love hamsters! Will you read next?"

Bethany looked pleased. "*Some* people appreciate the animal kingdom," she said.

"I love hamsters, too," Natalie said. "Remember?"

"They look like mice, and they have the IQ of a dust ball," Brianna said. Scowling, she took a mirror from her purse and applied colored gloss to her lips.

"Show-off!" Bethany muttered.

"Read your story," Hannah urged her again.

Bethany picked up her paper and began to read. " 'Blondie: Life of a Hamster . . .' "

"Hannah saves the day," Abby said proudly.

Everyone liked Hannah — if you didn't count Brianna, who only liked herself. Hannah never made enemies — only more and more friends. And Abby had been her first friend at Lancaster Elementary.

Chapter 3

Friday

"Honest criticism is the highest praise."

Tiny Toes Calendar

Then why wasn't Natalie pleased when I said her story was confusing?

I told her she had a great imagination. Her story, "Podo, Mouse of the North," was filled with exciting details, like marshmallow snow and swords that turned into dandelions. But so many things happened that I couldn't follow the story.

I gave Natalie honest criticism! Why didn't she realize it was the highest praise?

No one else in the group liked criticism, either.

When Brianna told Mason his story was gross and disgusting, he burped at her.

When Natalie told Bethany that her story was too short and that she should have  put in more action, like hamster fights, Bethany sulked.

Mason told me that my story was too perfect!! How can a story be <u>too</u> perfect???? Is that an insult or a compliment?

Only Hannah had something positive to say about everyone's work. She was the only person no one was mad at by the end of the writers group.

She didn't get mad at anyone, either.

Ms. Bunder says lots of writers are in writers groups. Is <u>this</u> what they're all like? Writers must be crazy.

The fifth-graders sat at their desks, decorating shoe boxes. The room was silent, except for the sound of rustling colored paper and scissors cutting.

Abby was smoothing purple paper onto the sides of her shoe box. After the gluing was done, she planned to add turquoise stars and white snowflakes.

Hannah was decorating her box with a collage of winter sports scenes from magazines. Mason was covering his box with the comics section of the newspaper. Bethany was cutting out pictures of animals and pasting them onto her box, which she had covered with green paper. Zach and Tyler were making their boxes look like computers. Natalie had gone wild with colors.

Brianna was decorating her box with silver and gold foil and shiny ribbons. It looked like it had been wrapped in a fancy store.

"Remember to write your name on the bottom of your box," Ms. Kantor reminded the class. "Not that you'll have any problem figuring out whose box is whose," she added. "Everyone's box is unique."

"Mine is the most unique," Brianna bragged, holding up a dazzling concoction in shiny foil.

"Ouch! It's so bright it hurts my eyes!" Mason yelled, holding his arm up to shield his face.

"How can the inside be as good as the outside?" Abby asked.

"It looks like a giant chocolate bar," Natalie said.

"My box is a precious treasure," Brianna insisted. "Whoever receives it will be the luckiest child in the world."

No one responded to her.

"I've got pictures of ice-skating, sledding, skiing, snowshoeing, and snowboarding on my box," Hannah announced. "Am I forgetting anything?"

"Ice fishing," Mason said.

"Snow angels," Bethany said.

"Reading," Abby suggested.

"That's a winter sport?" Zach said.

"Yes," Natalie said. "So are sleeping and hibernating."

Mason pretended to snore. Tyler folded a paper airplane and shot it at him.

"Settle down," Ms. Kantor said. "You need to finish your boxes and stack them up on the shelves."

There was a knock on the door. Ms. Yang, the school principal, hurried in. The class stared at her as she spoke to Ms. Kantor in a low voice. Ms. Yang didn't ordinarily come to their room. They saw her during assemblies and in the hallway at the beginning and end of the school day.

Ms. Kantor said a few words to Ms. Yang and then left the room.

"Continue with your activity," Ms. Yang said to the fifth-graders. "Ms. Kantor will return shortly."

Abby and Hannah exchanged glances.

"Ms. Yang! Is something wrong?" Natalie asked.

The principal didn't answer. She walked over to Brianna's desk and examined her box. "That's lovely, Brianna," she said.

Brianna smirked. "Of course, Ms. Yang."

"Look at mine!" Bethany called.

"Very creative," Ms. Yang said. She walked around the room, admiring everyone's boxes. "What are you going to do with them?"

Everyone rushed to answer.

"We're filling them with gifts," Hannah said.

"To send to children," Abby continued.

"Whose families don't have enough money," Natalie said.

"For the holidays," Mason finished.

"*Mine* is the best!" Brianna cried.

"What a wonderful project!" Ms. Yang said. "The boxes are a gift in themselves. Can I take pictures when you're done and display them at the entrance of the school?"

"Sure," everyone agreed.

"Now tell me what kinds of gifts you're putting inside," the principal said.

A dozen hands rose in the air at once, and then dropped as Ms. Kantor returned to the classroom.

Her face was pale and her eyes looked red.

"It's all right," she said to Ms. Yang's questioning glance. "Thank you."

Ms. Yang smiled at the fifth-graders. "Keep up the good work," she said. Then she left the room.

The class was silent as Ms. Kantor went to her desk and searched among her papers. Then she looked up at the students.

"You're unusually quiet right now," she observed with a small smile.

No one said anything.

"Here it is," Ms. Kantor said. She held up a note-book. "Lesson plans for the next month," she explained. She took a breath. "I just got news that my mother is sick and needs me to take care of her. I'll be out of school for a while."

"How long?" Tyler asked.

"I don't know," Ms. Kantor said. "It depends on how fast she recovers."

"Does that mean *substitutes*?" Natalie wailed.

Ms. Kantor looked stern. "Yes. I expect everyone to do their work and to be cooperative and helpful. Any more questions?"

"Will your mother be okay?" Mason asked.

"I hope so." Ms. Kantor smiled at Mason.

Brianna raised her hand. "What about our holiday project?" she asked.

"We need a responsible person in charge," their teacher said. "Someone to make regular announcements and to remind everyone to bring in gifts. Brianna? What about you?"

"I'm *much* too busy," Brianna said. "I have a lead role in the City Theater play, and I'm modeling every Saturday afternoon, and I'm . . ."

"Anyone else want to volunteer?" Ms. Kantor interrupted.

No one said anything.

"It's a fun job," Ms. Kantor said. "Maybe Ms. Bunder will distribute the boxes with whomever coordinates it. I can ask her if she'd be willing to help out."

"Ms. Bunder?!" Abby's hand shot up.

"Abby?" Ms. Kantor said. "Are you volunteering?"

"Um, yes," Abby said. "I think so."

"Good," Ms. Kantor said. "That's settled. Now, let's put away the boxes and get ready for science."

Chapter 4

Monday morning

"Nothing is often a good thing
to do and always a good thing
to say."

—Will Durant

Good Manners Calendar

OH, YEAH?

<u>If I Did Nothing and Said Nothing</u>
1. The shoe boxes would remain empty.
2. The kids wouldn't get their presents.
3. They wouldn't know that Ms. Kantor's class was thinking about them.
4. Their holidays wouldn't be as much fun.
5. Our class wouldn't have the satisfaction of making and sending gifts.
6. Ms. Kantor would be very disappointed.

Other Results of Doing and Saying Nothing

1. I wouldn't be friends with Hannah.
2. I'd never get my homework done.
3. I'd never answer questions in class.
4. I'd flunk fifth grade!!!

Wait! Does that mean I'd be in Ms. Bunder's class forever???? But if I did nothing, I'd never write anything for her assignments.

So there! Nothing isn't always a good thing to say or do. Something is better than nothing. Isn't that a saying, too?

Today I'm doing something.

I'm making my first announcement to remind everyone to bring in gifts.

Ms. Kantor told me I could suggest ideas for filling the boxes.

Ideas

1. Write a poem or letter to put in the box.
2. Put one of your favorite books in the box.

3. Put something handmade, like jewelry or a key chain, in the box.

Hooray! Ms. Kantor, Ms. Bunder, and Ms. Yang will be proud of me. Our boxes will be wonderful. The kids will love them.

I hope that we have Mrs. Diorio for a substitute again. Last time we had her, she read us a really exciting book for language arts, and she didn't give any homework. Everyone in the class liked her.

3:30 P.M.
I just reread today's quote: "Nothing is often a good thing to do and always a good thing to say."
This morning I thought the quote was stupid. Now I think it is <u>totally</u> true. I wish <u>everybody</u> took Will Durant's advice.
Especially Ms. Lee, our new substitute.

(What happened to Mrs. Diorio? She was so wonderful!!! <u>Why</u> wasn't she here today?)

Ms. Lee came into the classroom this morning just as the first bell rang.

She looked grouchy. She looked like she didn't want to be in our classroom. She looked like she wanted to be somewhere else, far away.

"Sit down!" she said. "Raise your hand when I call your name."

She read our names, one by one.

"Brianna," she said. Only she mispronounced it as "Brian-a."

"That's <u>Brianna</u>," Brianna corrected. "Lead actress, horseback rider, fashion model, winner of dozens of –"

"Zachary!" Ms. Lee barked.

"Call me Za –" Zach tried to say.

"Bethany! Mason! Natalie! Tyler! Why don't children have normal names anymore?" She frowned at us as if our names were our fault.

"Abigail!"

"I <u>hate</u> that name," I muttered.

"Quiet!" Ms. Lee said. "Hannah! Rachel! Jonathan!"

Natalie slid a piece of paper onto my desk. It said, "Ms. Lee is the _worst_!"

"That's for sure," I whispered.

"Silence!" Ms. Lee said. "Just because I'm a substitute, don't think you can take advantage of me."

"Ms. Kantor lets us talk," Mason bravely said.

"_I'm_ your teacher now," Ms. Lee said. "The rule is, No talking."

I raised my hand.

"And no questions!" Ms. Lee said. "Take out your math books and do page thirty-seven."

When I finished the math problems, I went up to Ms. Lee to ask if I could make the announcement about the gift boxes.

"Ms. Lee," I began.

"Sit down!" she said. "Finish your math!"

"But, I-"

"Did you hear me? Sit _down_!" she commanded.

"I need to-"

"Once more and I'm going to send you to the principal's office!" she said.

I went back to my seat. I felt like I couldn't breathe right.

Hannah gave me a sympathetic look. "It's not your fault," she said.

"She's <u>mean</u>," Natalie whispered.

"QUIET!" Ms. Lee said.

How am I supposed to remind everyone about bringing in gifts when the teacher won't let me make the announcement????

<u>It's not fair!!!</u>

I can't do my job. Will Ms. Kantor think it's my fault? Will the kids who were supposed to get our gift boxes be terribly disappointed? What am I going to do?????

<u>If Ms. Lee Had Said and Done Nothing</u>

1. She would not have come to school at all.

2. She wouldn't have yelled at us all day.

3. I would have made my announcement.
4. Our class would remember to bring in lots of gifts.
5. Everyone would be much happier!

I hope Ms. Lee won't be here tomorrow.

Chapter 5

Thursday

"Accept no substitutes."

The Real Thing Calendar

I wish we didn't have to accept any substitutes.

Ms. Lee is <u>still</u> in our classroom. She will be with us for the entire week — and maybe more. HELP!!!!

She is the worst substitute in the world. (Will give her a mention in the <u>Hayes Book of World Records</u>. Will also give my classmates an award for Brave Endurance of Unbearable Hardships.)

Ms. Lee does nothing but yell. We can't

Hayes Book of World Records

even raise our hands, except to answer questions. She won't listen to anyone.

Even Brianna is depressed. She says she can't stand to hear Ms. Lee say "Brian-a" one more time.

Mason got lunch detention for burping. He told Ms. Lee that it was a natural function, and she gave him a second detention. Now he has to spend two lunch periods indoors with <u>her</u>!

Mason wants to organize a classroom Burp-a-Thon. Will Ms. Lee give us <u>all</u> lunch detention? It won't be a punishment if the entire class is together.

We are practicing burping in our spare time. Mason is giving us pointers. Zach and Tyler are pretty good, Natalie can't burp at all, I'm only so-so, Hannah comes up with squeaks, and Brianna has talent.

"It's my stage training," she explained.

Our class is united. We have decided to burp together on Friday, after the school bell rings at the end of the day, as we file out the door.

But I still haven't made the announcement about the gift boxes.

I've tried to remind everyone personally, but it seems no one is listening.

My classmates say, "Yeah, sure," and then they forget. No one has brought in any gifts yet.

I understand: Everyone is upset about Ms. Lee. But the holidays are coming closer. What am I going to do? Maybe Ms. Bunder will help me out.

"Ms. Bunder is coming today!" Abby announced to a circle of friends on the playground before school. "I can't wait!!"

"Even kids who hate writing are going to be glad to see her after a few days of Ms. Lee," Natalie observed.

Bethany nodded in agreement.

"Who could hate writing in Ms. Bunder's class?" Abby wondered out loud. "Doesn't *everyone* love her?"

"*I* love her!" Hannah said.

"Ms. Bunder pronounces my name correctly," Brianna said.

"I wish Ms. Bunder was our permanent substitute," Bethany sighed. "We should ask Ms. Yang to hire her."

"Ms. Yang doesn't hire substitutes," Hannah said. "There's a special coordinator for that. My mother had to arrange for a long-term substitute when my little sister, Elena, was born."

"Ssshh! There she is!" Bethany whispered.

Everyone fell silent as Ms. Lee hurried past them.

"She doesn't even say hello," Natalie grumbled.

Hannah suddenly broke away from the group. "Hello, Ms. Lee!" she called in a friendly voice.

Ms. Lee looked startled. "Hello," she said, then ducked inside the school.

"Saying hello to the enemy?" Natalie demanded. "How could you?"

Hannah looked uncomfortable. "She's just a . . ."

"Mean and nasty witch?" Natalie finished.

"She's never heard of City Theater!" Brianna said indignantly.

"She's the worst person in the world," Bethany agreed.

Everyone was staring at Hannah.

"I thought she'd be friendlier if I said hello," Hannah explained.

"It was a good idea," Abby said slowly.

Natalie frowned. "Just remember how mean she is. Nothing's going to change that."

"Get out blank paper for the spelling quiz," Ms. Lee told the class. "Clear your desks off, and *no talking.*"

"Do you have an extra pencil?" Hannah whispered to Abby. "Mine broke."

Ms. Lee scowled at the two girls. "You! Abigail and Hannah! Stop it *now*! Or you'll both get a zero on the quiz."

Abby ripped a sheet of paper from her notebook. *It isn't fair*, she thought furiously. *We weren't even talking. Hannah just needed a pencil.*

She dropped a pencil on the floor and kicked it toward Hannah. Hannah leaned over to pick it up. Fortunately, Ms. Lee didn't notice.

"All right. Listen carefully. I'm not repeating myself. There are twenty words in this quiz. Write the numbers one through twenty on your paper now," Ms. Lee ordered.

The door to the classroom opened. Ms. Bunder walked in.

Every student in the class turned toward her in anticipation.

"Hello, I'm Ms. Bunder, the creative writing teacher." She held out her hand to Ms. Lee.

Ms. Lee stared at her suspiciously. "Creative writing teacher? You're not on the schedule."

Ms. Bunder shook her head. "Ms. Kantor was so upset about her mother, it must have slipped her mind to tell you. I come in every Thursday to do a special creative writing workshop with the class."

"Hooray!" Abby cried. "She does, and it's great!"

"*Quiet!*" Ms. Lee snapped. "I heard nothing about a creative writing class. We're having a spelling quiz right now. Please leave the classroom."

"But, Ms. Kantor —" Ms. Bunder began.

"Left me no note," Ms. Lee finished. "I repeat: Creative writing is not on the schedule. You are interrupting the lesson plan."

"*Excuse* me," Ms. Bunder said, then glanced at the class. She seemed about to say something else. Instead she pressed her lips tightly together, turned, and walked out of the classroom.

Chapter 6

Friday

"More than enough is
too much."

—Thomas Fuller

Milkshake Calendar

My class has had more than enough of
Ms. Lee.

We have had too much of Ms. Lee.

We have had <u>way too much</u> of Ms.
Lee.

(Even Hannah, who likes <u>everyone</u>, has
had too much of Ms. Lee.)

Everyone was shocked when Ms. Lee
wouldn't let Ms. Bunder teach creative
writing.

I was <u>furious</u>! As Ms. Bunder walked

out the door, I did something unexpected. I jumped out of my seat.

"Ms. Lee!" I cried. "Ms. Bunder comes in every week! You can't just send her away—"

"I'm in charge here. Back in your chair <u>now</u>," Ms. Lee ordered, "or take an automatic zero on the quiz."

I couldn't move for a moment. Then, suddenly, I sat down.

My hands were trembling. My face was hot. Hannah nudged me in sympathy.

"Nice try," she whispered.

Ms. Lee started reading off the quiz words. I could barely concentrate. If it had been a math quiz, I would have gotten a zero anyway. As it was, I missed six words that I knew.

After school, all my friends told me I was brave for standing up for Ms. Bunder. But it didn't bring her back to our class.

I wonder what Ms. Bunder did after she left the classroom. She looked upset. I've never seen her look upset before. Did she go home? Did she complain to Ms. Yang? I hope so! Will she come back next week? Or will she stay away until Ms. Kantor returns?

Everyone is disappointed!!! We all miss Ms. Bunder <u>sooooooo</u> much! If she made us do writers groups for the rest of the year, <u>no one</u> would complain! We'd even be happy to do constructive criticism again!

Someone should give Ms. Lee constructive criticism. Like, try smiling once in a while. Get our names right. And don't yell all day long. Kids are not your enemies.

Finally, Ms. Lee, let <u>me</u> remind everyone about the gift boxes.

<u>Help!</u> What am I going to do? Now that Ms. Bunder is gone, so is my last hope of making an announcement to the class.

<u>Later</u>:
Hooray for Hannah! I confided my problem to her, and <u>she came up with the perfect solution</u>.

Hannah accompanied me to Ms. Yang's

office after school. She waited while I asked Ms. Yang if I could make the gift box announcement during morning messages.

Ms. Yang said she was happy to help our project. She said I could make the announcement Friday morning.

That's today!! I am SO nervous!!! I've got to make a dramatic announcement. Not only will the entire school hear what I say, but this may be my one chance to remind our class to bring in their gifts.

"Good morning, students," Ms. Yang said into the microphone of the loudspeaker system. "Please stand for the Pledge."

After the students recited the Pledge of Allegiance, she continued. "It's Friday morning. Happy birthday to our school custodian, Mr. Morris, and to two kindergarten students, Jenna and Kelsey. Remember to get your birthday ice cream at the cafeteria today.

"We have a special announcement this morning," Ms. Yang continued. She motioned Abby forward. "Listen carefully, everyone, to Abby Hayes."

Abby stepped up to the microphone. Her heart was pounding. She took a breath to calm herself and then began to speak. "Ms. Kantor's class is collecting gifts to send to underprivileged kids for the holidays," she said. "This is a reminder to everyone in Ms. Kantor's class to bring them in. The gifts have to be small enough to fit in a shoe box."

Abby paused for a moment. "Many people don't have enough money to buy food or clothing for their families. Their kids don't have presents over the holidays. Just imagine how these kids will feel when they open our packages. Our gifts will say that we care. A small gift can make a big difference!"

Abby stopped. "Um, thank you. And don't forget, Ms. Kantor's class. Bring your gifts in next week."

"Thank *you*, Abby." Ms. Yang smiled at her. "That was very inspiring. If anyone else wants to donate gifts for this project, bring them to Ms. Kantor's fifth-grade class. Abby is in charge."

"I'm the one with the curly red hair," Abby blurted, "who usually wears purple."

"Have a good day," Ms. Yang told the students in closing.

The principal turned off the microphone. "I'll give you a note so you won't get marked late," she said to Abby.

"Thank you," Abby said to Ms. Yang. *And thank you, Hannah*, she added silently.

"Come back next week, and remind everyone again," Ms. Yang told her. "Once is never enough."

"I will!" Abby sighed with relief. Then she gathered up her courage to ask the question that she had wanted to ask since entering the principal's office.

"Is Ms. Bunder going to teach creative writing next week?" she asked.

"I'm sorry, Abby." The principal picked up paper and pen. "Ms. Bunder can't teach until Ms. Kantor returns, I'm afraid," Ms. Yang said.

"You mean, Ms. Lee can kick her out?" Abby said in shock.

Ms. Yang shook her head. "It's not a matter of being kicked out. Ms. Bunder does the writing workshops by private arrangement with Ms. Kantor. She's not a school employee."

"Oh," Abby said in a small voice. "But Ms. Kantor said that Ms. Bunder might help distribute the gift boxes."

"I'll help you," Ms. Yang offered.

"Thank you," Abby said again. She hoped she didn't sound as disappointed as she felt.

"I know how special Ms. Bunder is," Ms. Yang said sympathetically.

She scrawled a few words on the paper and

handed it to Abby. "Hurry back to your classroom," she said. "And be patient. Ms. Kantor will return, and so will Ms. Bunder."

A debate raged on the playground at recess.

"To burp or not to burp, that is the question," Mason recited. He punctuated his remark with a loud one.

"Eight point seven," Tyler said. He had started rating burps on a scale from one to ten.

"You're lucky Ms. Lee didn't hear that," Abby said to Mason. "She'd have given you lunch detention again."

"Here's burping at you, kid," Mason said.

"We'll all be doing it together at the end of school today," Natalie said with satisfaction. Her burping ability had improved that week from a one point five to a six. "We'll see what Ms. Lee will do then!"

Many fifth-graders cheered in agreement.

"I don't think this is a good idea," Hannah said for about the sixth time. "Ms. Lee will be even angrier. . . ."

Natalie ignored her. "Maybe she'll quit."

"*Yes!*" Bethany cried.

"The Burp-a-Thon might backfire," Hannah persisted. "What if Ms. Yang hears about it?" She looked to Abby for support.

"I —" Abby began.

"Ms. Yang *will* hear about it!" Brianna affirmed. "She'll hear the sound of freedom, truth, and justice ringing out." She checked to see if everyone was listening. "That's a line from my last starring role."

"I think . . ." Abby tried again.

"Never mind that," Natalie interrupted. "Let's practice coordinating our burps."

"Ms. Yang will be really upset," Hannah insisted. "Do we want the principal mad at us? And then Ms. Kantor will be so disappointed. . . ."

"So?" Zach said.

Natalie put her hands on her hips and stared at Hannah. "What happened to you?" she said. "You used to be on our side."

"I *am* on your side," Hannah insisted. "I just think we should change the plan."

"To *what*?" Natalie demanded.

Hannah leaned close and whispered in her ear.

Natalie's frown slowly disappeared. It was replaced with a wide smile.

"Yes!" she cried. "That's *it*!"

Chapter 7

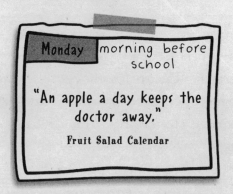

Monday morning before school

"An apple a day keeps the doctor away."

Fruit Salad Calendar

Will an apple a day keep the <u>substitute teacher</u> away??

What about thirty apples? Or forty? Or sixty?

We are all bringing apples to Ms. Lee today. Every kid in Ms. Kantor's fifth-grade class is bringing in at least one, and maybe two or three or even four apples. We will place them on Ms. Lee's desk all day long.

We're going to pretend it's a coincidence.

The Avalanche of Apples is about to begin!!!

It's the perfect plot, and Hannah thought it up herself. I can't believe that she convinced <u>everyone</u>, even Natalie and Mason and Brianna, to change from Plan Burp to Plan Apple.

Does she have magic powers?

Or is it "natural leadership ability"? (That's what my older sisters have. But Hannah is much nicer than Eva and Isabel.)

Hooray for Hannah! I'm so proud that she's my friend!

"Did everyone bring their apples?" Hannah asked her classmates on Monday morning as they stood outside on the playground, waiting for the first bell to ring and the school doors to open.

Everyone nodded. Some of them patted bulging pockets; others pointed to their backpacks.

"I brought imported apples," Brianna announced. "One of them is as big as a grapefruit."

"Mine are small and cheap," Mason said.

"I *almost* ate mine for breakfast," Bethany said. "But then I remembered it was for Ms. Lee."

"Watch out!" Abby warned. "Teacher alert!"

Ms. Lee strode down the sidewalk. She was wearing a bulky winter coat and a fleece cap. Her mouth was turned down in a permanent scowl. She walked with a heavy step.

"Don't smile!" Natalie ordered the others in a low voice. "Keep a straight face!"

"I can't!" Hannah wailed. "I *have* to smile!"

"She does," Abby agreed.

"All right, everyone *except* Hannah keep a straight face," Natalie amended. "Or at least act normal."

Mason burped loudly.

"*Stop!*" Brianna said. "You're *disgusting*!"

"Yes, we're acting normal," Abby said to Hannah, who started to laugh.

"*Ssssh!*" Bethany said. "Here she comes!"

Ms. Lee yanked open the front door and stomped into the school.

"Looks like she's in an even better mood than usual," Natalie observed sarcastically.

"Who's firing the first apple?" one of the boys asked.

"Firing?" Hannah pulled a bright red apple out

of her pocket. "This is an apple of *peace*."

"Mine is a cannonball," Zach said.

"A bowling ball," Jonathan said. "Strike!"

"*Whatever,*" Brianna said.

"Hannah should be first!" Abby said. "The Apple Avalanche was her idea!"

Natalie didn't look pleased. Neither did Brianna.

"I don't *have* to be first," Hannah said uncomfortably. "Does anyone else want to place the first apple on Ms. Lee's desk?"

"No, I'll be second," Brianna said, with a wave of her hand. "Even though I'm *usually* first."

"Natalie?"

"Oh, it's all right. Hannah can do it," Natalie grumbled, "since she has all the *great* ideas."

Hannah glanced at Abby. Then she shrugged. "Well, if you're sure about it," she said.

"Do it!" Mason boomed.

"What do we do if, you know, I mean, you know, what if, if, if . . ." Bethany's voice trailed off.

"*What?*" Brianna said.

"If — if we get into trouble, and Ms. Yang calls our parents?" Bethany finished.

The kids looked at one another nervously.

Hannah took a breath. "We'll say it's a school tradition," she said. "An apple to the teacher on the second Monday after Thanksgiving."

Everyone filed into the school in an apprehensive silence. Abby kept her hand in her coat pocket. She had brought two Granny Smith apples. They were green and tart — like Ms. Lee, she thought.

Ms. Lee had hung up her coat and was writing the day's assignments on the blackboard.

"No talking!" she barked as they entered the room. "Hang up your coats, go to your seats, and take out your notebooks! *Without a word!*"

Hannah placed her finger on her lips, tiptoed to the teacher's desk, and left a shiny red apple there.

One after another, everyone silently placed their apples on the desk.

"What's *this*??" Ms. Lee said, turning around as Mason left a tiny yellow apple on the corner of the desk.

"Um . . . an apple for the teacher," Mason said.

Ms. Lee stared at the apples piled up on her desk. "It's more than *an* apple," she snapped. "There are at least thirty here. Are these all from *you*?"

He shook his head.

Ms. Lee looked around the classroom. Her gaze rested on each student.

"Is this some kind of practical joke?" she demanded.

No one moved or said a word. Abby's heart pounded. She didn't dare look at her friends.

"*You!*" Ms. Lee said, pointing to Brianna. "Brian-a. Get me a bag and put the apples in it."

"Bri-*an*na," Brianna said under her breath.

"The rest of you prepare for science," Ms. Lee ordered.

She stood at the blackboard, muttering to herself.

Abby opened her binder and took out a pen. Her classmates did the same. The room was quiet.

At the teacher's desk, Brianna placed the apples, one after another, into a paper bag. Every few moments, she sighed dramatically.

"Brian-a! Sit down! That's enough!" Ms. Lee commanded.

The students exchanged glances. There were still a couple of apples on the desk. What was Ms. Lee going to do next?

"Pens in hand," Ms. Lee ordered. "Paper on desk. Eyes on paper."

Hannah leaned over and whispered in Abby's ear. "Everyone should keep leaving apples on her desk all day. Until we run out. Pass it on."

"Are you *crazy*?" Abby whispered back. "Haven't we gone far enough?"

"Pass it on!" Hannah repeated urgently.

"*QUIET!*" Ms. Lee glared at the students, as if challenging them to argue with her. Then she picked up an apple and bit into it.

Chapter 8

Monday | Apple Monday

"Too much is seldom enough."

—J. C. Hare and A. W. Hare

Pocket Calendar of Mice, Ants, and Flies

<u>Oh, yeah?</u>

Our class has had too much of Ms. Lee <u>and</u> enough of her, too.

Ms. Lee has had too much of our Apple Avalanche <u>and</u> enough of it, too.

We kept putting apples on her desk all day.

Ms. Lee kept making Brianna put them in bags.

(Brianna has had too much apple packing <u>and</u> enough of it, too.)

At the end of the day, Brianna rebelled. She refused to put another apple in another bag.

"I won't!" she said.

"You're the ringleader, aren't you?" Ms. Lee said. "I know your type. You can't fool me. Pack up those apples right now, or go to the principal's office."

"You are cruel, unfair, and unjust!" Brianna cried, as if she were reciting lines from a play. (She probably was.)

Hannah stood up. "I'm the ringlead —" she tried to say.

Ms. Lee and Brianna both ignored her.

They faced each other, glaring.

"My aunt's brother-in-law's cousin's uncle's girlfriend's mother is on the school board." There were two bright red circles on Brianna's cheeks. "I'm going to register a complaint about you! And my name is Brianna, not Brian-a!"

Ms. Lee said nothing. Suddenly, she grabbed an apple and smashed it on the floor. Then she picked up her coat and stomped out of the room.

Our class sat in shocked silence. No one could even look at anyone else.

"Boy, she flipped out," Mason finally said.

We all laughed nervously.

"Talk about a temper!" Bethany said.

"Did you see her throw that apple?" Zach said admiringly.

"It was aimed at _me_!" Brianna proclaimed. "I'm going to _sue_!"

Just then, Ms. Yang walked into the classroom.

Ms. Yang asked us to tell her what happened. We told her the entire story (except that there were so many apples). She looked _very_ upset, especially when Brianna told her how Ms. Lee had thrown the apple. But she wasn't mad at us. She said Ms. Lee would not return to school tomorrow.

Everyone in the class tried very hard to keep a straight face.

(Straight? Our faces were strange. We were trying so hard not to smile, laugh, and cheer.)

I can cheer as much as I want in my journal. Hooray!!! Hooray!!! Hooray!!!

Ms. Lee is gone. She won't return!!! And she's NEVER coming back!

Chapter 9

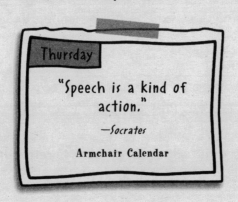

It is!!!

Ms. Yang let me make announcements every morning this week. I talked about kids whose families didn't have enough money to buy them gifts. I said that Ms. Kantor's class would show them that they weren't forgotten. I asked everyone to imagine the happy and surprised looks on the kids' faces when they received our presents.

My speech did something unexpected.

Everyone in Ms. Kantor's class brought in gifts to fill their shoe boxes, and so did the rest of the school.

We now have hundreds of gifts! There are bags of presents on the shelves at the back of the classroom. There are bags in the coatroom. There are bags in Ms. Yang's office.

I never knew that words could create so much action!

We have received key chains, small stuffed animals, books, notepads, gel pens, socks, pencils, dolls, fleece hats, bracelets, paint sets, balls, crayons, CDs, and games.

A few days ago, we had an Apple Avalanche. Now we have a Gift Avalanche!

"'O, Romeo, Romeo!' " Isabel cried.

Abby's older sister tossed the book onto the desk. "Phooey," she said.

"You were good." Abby sat cross-legged on Isabel's bed.

Isabel sighed dramatically. "I have to perform the

scene with Peter as Romeo. He's six inches shorter than I am, and he has big teeth."

"Do you have to kiss him?" Abby asked.

"Ugh! NO!" Isabel cried. "Thank goodness, it's just a classroom reading."

She sat down across from Abby. "Speaking of classrooms, how's school without Ms. Kantor?"

"We've had a different substitute for each of the last three days," Abby said. "None of them were as mean as Ms. Lee."

Isabel shook her head. "Last year we had a substitute who covered up all the clocks with sheets of paper and wouldn't give anyone a pass for the bathroom."

"Yikes," Abby said. "That sounds even worse than Ms. Lee."

Isabel looked at her fingernails, which she had painted sparkling silver. "Do you like this color?" she asked Abby. "Or should I change it?"

"Your fingernails look like spaceships," Abby said. "Or glitter wrap."

"Spaceships?" Isabel said. "Glitter wrap?"

Abby shrugged. "I guess I have gift boxes on my mind," she explained. She told Isabel about the project. "Since I made the announcements, we've received hundreds of presents."

"Congratulations! That's great!" Isabel said admiringly. "What are you going to do with all of them?"

"Donate them to a children's charity, I guess," Abby said hesitantly. "It'll be too complicated to make more gift boxes."

"Especially without Ms. Kantor to organize it," Isabel agreed.

"On the news, they said that the police are collecting new, unwrapped gifts to give to kids. Do you think that's a good idea?" Abby asked.

"Terrific!" Isabel said. "It sounds like a perfect solution."

"You mean that?" Abby said. It wasn't often that her older sister praised her.

"It's almost like one of *my* ideas." Isabel picked up her book of Shakespeare's plays. "Time to rehearse again. Once more, with feeling."

" 'O, Romeo, Romeo!' " she cried. " 'Wherefore art thou Romeo?' "

Abby stood up to leave. "Romeo's at the mall, checking out electronic games," she said. "Juliet's having her ears pierced —"

"You've got it wrong," Isabel corrected her. " 'Wherefore art thou Romeo?' means 'Why are you named Romeo?' *Not* 'Where are you, Romeo?' "

"What*ever*," Abby said. "It's just a *joke*." She fled the room before her sister delivered a lecture on Shakespeare, Romeo, and the English language.

"This is the *greatest* series!" Bethany exclaimed to her friends. They were on the playground at lunch recess. She held up a blue paperback book with a picture of a girl and a hamster on the cover.

"*Book One: Dilly's Dash for Freedom*," she read. "It's all about a girl and her pets. Each book features a different animal."

"I read the entire Perfect Pet series," Natalie said. "It's the best. Except that no one ever gets any older."

Abby groaned. "I *hate* that! They have a million summer vacations and then they're back in the same grade again. I bet Shakespeare never did that."

"Shakespeare?" Bethany said. "Did he write series?"

"There's a horse called Juliet in the fifth Perfect Pet book," Hannah said. "That was my favorite one."

"Me, too!" Natalie practically jumped up and down with excitement. "Remember when Juliet . . ."

"Don't spoil it!" Bethany cried. "I haven't even finished the first one yet!"

"Those Perfect Pet books are *sooooooo* dumb!" Mason said.

"Shut up, Mason," Natalie said.

"Speaking of dumb books," he continued, "someone donated a box of Perfect Pet books to our gift drive. Ms. Yang made me take them upstairs to the classroom."

"We're drowning in presents!" Hannah cried.

"How many do we have?" Bethany asked.

"Oh, a billion or so," Natalie said.

"At *least*," Mason agreed.

"What are we going to do with all of them?" Brianna asked.

"I have a *great* plan," Abby announced confidently. If Isabel liked her idea, her classmates would, too. "The police department is doing a holiday gift drive," she said. "We can bring the extra gifts to them. We won't even have to wrap them. That's the simplest solution."

"Do we *want* simple?" Natalie asked with a frown.

"Well," Abby began, "since Ms. Kantor isn't here . . ."

"I like Abby's idea," Hannah said. "Let's do it."

Brianna spoke up. "Before we decide anything, you should know that my mother's cousin's brother-in-law is a reporter for the newspaper."

"And my grandfather's aunt's next-door neighbor's dog is mayor of the city," Mason retorted.

"The mayor is related to *me*," Brianna said. "The dog is *you*."

Mason burped.

"He thought our project would make a great article, and he mentioned it to the features editor," Brianna continued. "A reporter is coming to our school next week with a *professional* photographer."

"Great!" Natalie cried. "Brianna, you're the best!"

"I am," Brianna agreed.

"That's great, but it still doesn't solve the problem of the extra presents," Abby said. "Let's take them to the police station."

"One or two people should not be making *all* the decisions," Natalie said pointedly. "We need to make more gift boxes. That's what the kids in our school gave us gifts for."

"But we've already made one box each," Hannah

argued. "Isn't that enough? It's okay if we donate the extra gifts to a good cause."

"It isn't," Natalie insisted.

"Making more boxes is too much work," Abby protested.

"I *told* the newspaper that we're doing gift boxes," Brianna interrupted. "They thought it was the *best* idea."

"Ms. Kantor would be thrilled if we made more than twenty-five gift boxes," Bethany added. "Wouldn't that be a nice welcome back?"

"YES!" Natalie said.

Other kids nodded in agreement.

Abby shrugged. "If that's what everyone wants to do, it's okay with me. But we'd have to get permission from the substitutes." She looked at her friends. "That might not be easy."

"So?" Natalie said.

"I don't mind," Bethany chimed in. "I've cleaned stables. I've rehearsed gymnastics routines for months at a time. That's a *lot* harder."

"When will we make the new boxes?" Mason said. "Recess? After school? During class?"

"It depends on the substitute," Abby said again.

Natalie scowled at her. She seemed about to say

something, but Hannah interrupted.

"I have an idea!" she cried. "You can all come to my house this weekend, and we'll decorate boxes in my basement. I'll ask my mother — I'm sure she'll say yes. We won't have to worry about substitutes."

Everyone cheered.

"Hooray!" Bethany cried. "I'll be there."

"Me, too," Natalie said, smiling again.

"Eerp," Mason said.

"This weekend I have play rehearsals, French and violin lessons, shopping, and an awards dinner," Brianna sighed. "But I'll fit it in *somehow*."

"It's settled, then." Hannah looked relieved. She glanced at Abby. "You'll help, won't you, Abby? I won't do it without you."

"Of course," Abby said.

Chapter 10

"A friend is a second self."
—Aristotle

Sharing and Caring Calendar

Is Hannah my second self, or am I hers? We're now partners on the gift box project. My announcements brought in the gifts, and Hannah will manage the box decorating. That includes reminding everyone to bring supplies to her house this weekend.

<u>Phew!!!</u> I'm glad, overjoyed, thrilled, happy, and relieved that organizing the boxes is <u>NOT</u> my responsibility.

We'll all bring shoe boxes, wrapping paper, and glue to Hannah's house at one o'clock this afternoon. We'll work together until the boxes are done.

Hannah's mother will bring the boxes to school on Monday, and we'll fill them at recess. After the newspaper reporter visits, we will deliver the completed gift boxes to Ms. Yang. Ms. Yang will distribute them to different families in time for the holidays. Instead of twenty or thirty kids receiving our gifts, there'll be more than <u>one hundred</u> who will have a happier holiday because of us!!!

"Come in, Abby." Hannah's mother, Susan, opened the front door. Hannah's baby sister, Elena, peeked out from behind her legs.

"AAAaaaaaa!" Elena shrieked.

"She's scared of all the new, unfamiliar faces," Susan explained.

"Mine is old and familiar." Abby crouched down and smiled at Elena. "Hi, Elena! Hi! Hi! You know me! It's Abby!"

Elena stared at her. She had a smear of jam on her face and a purple plastic watering can in her hand. "Wa-ta," she said. "Fwowa."

"Fwowa?" Abby repeated.

"We're going to water the houseplants together," Susan explained. "Elena loves to water flowers. She's my helper."

"And I'm your friend," Abby said. "Abby! Can you say 'Abby'?"

"Babby!" Elena answered.

"You said it!" Abby cried. She stood up. "She is *sooooooo* cute. I wish I had a little sister!"

"Hannah will lend her out," Susan said. "She might even pay you to take her."

She led Abby into the kitchen.

"Everyone's in the basement," Susan said, pointing to the door. "They're waiting for you."

"Me!" Elena said. She started crawling backward down the stairs. Her mother scooped her up.

"No!" Elena screamed.

"Let's water plants, Elena. Isn't that fun?" Susan carried a kicking, protesting Elena out of the room.

Abby closed the door behind her and went downstairs.

Ten fifth-graders sat around a long table, gluing colored paper onto boxes.

"Welcome to Basement Boxes, Inc.," Hannah

joked. "Where ordinary shoe boxes are transformed into extraordinary . . ."

"Shoe boxes," Mason finished.

"So, how many did you bring?" Zach asked. "You're not allowed to leave until you wrap your quota."

"Just three, right?" Abby said, opening her bag and taking out the boxes she had found in the attic.

"At *least*," Natalie said. She had already covered one box with paper rockets and another with glittery stars. "A lot of kids didn't show up."

Abby sat down on a folding chair. "I thought the entire class was coming."

"Rachel has a stomach virus, Tyler has hockey, and it's Jonathan's weekend with his father," Hannah recited. "I don't know where Brianna is."

"It's just us and the boxes," Mason grumbled.

"But we have popcorn," Hannah said cheerfully, pointing to a big bowl on the table. "Watch out! It's greasy!"

Mason picked up some plain wrapping paper. "I could decorate this with my thumbprints," he suggested.

"We'll send them to the police department," Natalie joked.

Abby glanced at the pile of unwrapped shoe boxes. "How long will it take eleven of us to wrap all of those?"

"Too long," Mason said.

"I brought horses, cats, dogs, birds, lizards, bugs, fish, snakes, and elephants," Bethany announced. "Every possible kind of animal wrapping paper!"

"It's a zoo!" Zach cried.

Abby took out a bunch of multicolored bows and rolls of shiny ribbon from her bag. "I thought we could use these, too."

"Great!" Hannah cried. "We'll make the most beautiful packages ever!"

Abby stood up and stretched. Her fingers were sticky with glue. "After today, I never want to decorate another box!" she cried. "Especially those lids!"

"They're the worst," Natalie agreed. "The corners are hard to get straight."

"Fifty-nine, sixty, sixty-one . . ." Hannah counted the boxes. "We've done sixty-seven!" she announced. "Let's take a break!"

The basement door opened. At the top of the stairs, Susan said, "Go right down, girls."

"I wonder who's here," Natalie said.

"Why are we, like, doing this?" an irritated voice asked.

"I *promised*," someone else replied in a loud whisper. "It'll just take a few minutes. I'll wrap a box or two, and then we'll go."

Brianna and her best friend, Victoria, appeared at the bottom of the stairs.

"Hello, all!" Brianna cried in her television voice. She was wearing shiny blue pants and a white coat with a fur collar. "Guess what? I'm here to help! And look who I brought with me!"

Victoria made a face. She was wearing tight black pants and a pink sheepskin coat. "Like, I'm not going to, like, get my hands dirty or anything," she said.

"We're going to be *featured* in the newspaper!" Brianna hissed at her friend. She smiled brightly at her classmates. "Why are you all just sitting around?"

"We're taking a break," Zach said. He pointed to the boxes. "We've already wrapped sixty-seven."

"Good work, team." Brianna slipped off her coat and sat down next to Bethany. "I'll finish this one," she said, picking up a box that was half covered with iguanas.

"That's mine!" Bethany cried.

"You mean I have to start a whole new one?" Brianna said. "Oh, all right." She took a plain box and began to wrap it in pink paper.

For a few moments, the room was quiet.

"All done!" Brianna announced. She held up the box for everyone to admire.

Victoria tapped her foot impatiently.

"You forgot to wrap the lid," Natalie pointed out.

"The lid?" Brianna repeated.

Victoria stood up and headed for the stairs. "I'm not waiting around for, like, a *lid*," she said. "I have, like, important shopping to do, you know."

Brianna dropped the pink box and rushed after Victoria. "Bye, all!" she called. "Don't thank me! It was nothing, really!"

The remaining kids exchanged glances.

"It really *was* nothing," Natalie said to Brianna's retreating back. "Why did you, like, even bother?"

Chapter 11

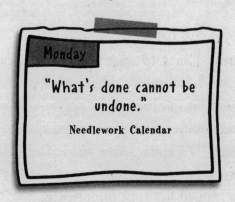

Monday

"What's done cannot be undone."

Needlework Calendar

Hooray!!!!

What's Done

82-1/2 boxes (67 before Brianna arrived; 1/2 while she was there; 15 after she left)

What It Took to Get Them Done

3 hours and 37 minutes of work

15 glue sticks, 8 pairs of scissors, 57 bows, lots of wrapping paper

4 plates of cookies, 1 huge bowl of popcorn, 2 quarts of juice

＊　＊　＊

None of this can be undone. Not even Brianna's pink half-box. Thank goodness!!!!

After everyone left, I stayed at Hannah's house for a sleepover. We watched a movie after dinner, ate more popcorn, and played games until 11 o'clock, when her mother said, "Lights out!"

Hannah's room has rainbow wallpaper. She has a tropical fish mobile, lots of books, a fake fur rug, and her own telephone.

She told me about her best friend in her old school. Her name is Sophie. Now that Hannah has moved away, they don't see each other much anymore. When they do see each other, it's not as much fun.

I told Hannah about my former best friend, Jessica, who moved away to live with her father and his new family. She has changed a lot since then. Now we don't have much in common.

Hannah and I agreed that moving is hard on friendships. When one person isn't there anymore, it's not easy to stay close.

When the lights went out, we kept on talking. In the dark, it was easy to tell secrets. I told Hannah one.

"I wish my older sisters weren't so perfect!" I said. "I hate being compared to them."

Hannah sympathized. "That must be awful." Then she told me her secret. "At my old school, there were some kids who didn't like me."

"Wow," I said. "That's hard to imagine."

"They really didn't like me," Hannah confided. "They were even trying to get Sophie to turn against me."

I didn't know what to say. I just listened.

Then Hannah told me another secret. She's afraid that the kids here won't like her, either.

"Are you crazy?" I said. "Everyone likes you."

"Really?" She sounded surprised.

"You've come up with some of the greatest ideas the fifth grade has ever known," I said. "I'm going to give you a double page

in the <u>Hayes Book of World Records</u>.
Brianna's the only other fifth-grader who
has one."

"<u>Brianna?</u>"

"For World-class Boast-a-thons," I explained. "When it comes to bragging, Brianna <u>is</u> the best."

Hannah laughed. Then she got serious
again. "You're <u>sure</u> no one's mad at me?"

"Yes," I said.

"<u>Good</u>," Hannah said.

When Abby arrived at school Monday morning, Hannah and her mother had already brought in forty-five of the gift boxes. They were piled at the back of the room, ready to be filled with donated gifts.

Abby smiled and waved to Hannah.

Hannah didn't smile back.

"Wait until Ms. Kantor hears what a great job we did!" Abby said. "Wait until all the kids open their holiday presents!"

"Yeah, sure," Hannah muttered.

Abby stared at her friend. "Is something wrong?" she asked.

"I — " Hannah began.

"Aren't there a lot more boxes?" Natalie interrupted. "I thought we did twice as many."

"My orange-and-purple box is missing," Mason said. "I wanted to fill it with plastic lizards."

"It's, uh, still at my house," Hannah said carefully. "I'll bring it later."

"Okay, sure." Mason shrugged. "Whatever."

"You couldn't take all the boxes in one trip?" Natalie asked. "No big deal. Bring the rest tomorrow."

Hannah seemed about to say something, then stopped. The first bell rang. The fifth-graders hurried to their desks.

Abby took out her journal and opened it on her lap. A new substitute teacher came into the room. He was a young man, but he was already balding. He wore corduroy pants and a light blue sweater. His face was friendly.

"Hi, my name is Mr. Weston," he introduced himself.

Concealing her journal underneath the desk, Abby began to write.

Mr. Weston is our new substitute.
Mr. Weston _seems_ nice.

Mr. Weston is passing out books. We are going to divide into reading groups.

Later:
Mr. Weston _is_ nice.

Even later:
Mr. Weston is <u>definitely</u> nice!

At recess, we filled boxes with gifts. That was fun! (And a lot faster than wrapping them.)

When Mr. Weston saw all the gifts and boxes, he asked what we were doing. When we told him, he offered to help!!! He packed boxes with us at recess and gave us good suggestions, like making separate boxes for older and younger kids.

We told him about the photographer and the news reporter. He said he hoped he was in our class that day.

I do, too! Mr. Weston is the best substitute we've had so far. Hooray!!

The only thing left to worry about is

Hannah. She looks upset. It can't be the boxes. No one cares if she didn't bring them all in at once.

<u>What's wrong?????</u>

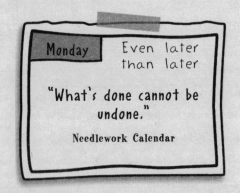

Monday   Even later
          than later

"What's done cannot be
undone."

Needlework Calendar

<u>Oh, yeah????</u>

I just found out what Hannah is worrying about.

She wouldn't tell me right away.
I had to promise never to tell anyone, <u>ever</u>.
I held up my hand. "Scout's honor," I said. "Even though I'm not a Scout."

Hannah <u>still</u> didn't tell me. She said it

was the most awful, terrible tragedy . . .

. . . AND the most rotten, horrible event in the history of mankind.

She swore I'd have to give it an entire chapter in the <u>Hayes Book of World Records</u>.

"Okay, I will!" I promised. "Just tell me already!"

Hannah took a deep breath.

"Elena did it," she began.

"Elena did what?" I asked.

"You won't believe it," Hannah said.

"What could that precious little baby do?" I asked.

"<u>Precious little baby?</u> She's more destructive than a cyclone, hurricane, and volcano put together!"

Hannah put her head close to mine and whispered. "She crawled down the stairs into the basement."

"So?" I said.

"<u>And she single-handedly destroyed half the boxes!</u>"

Chapter 12

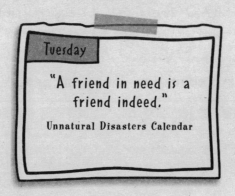

> Tuesday
>
> **"A friend in need is a friend indeed."**
>
> **Unnatural Disasters Calendar**

I couldn't speak for several minutes.
I was in shock.
"She did?" I finally squeaked.
"Yes," Hannah said. "She did."

Hannah told me all the details. I still couldn't speak.

<u>What One Baby Did</u>
1. Crawled downstairs.
2. Found purple watering can filled with water.

3. "Watered" boxes until 37-1/2 of them were a runny, soggy mush.

It's hard to believe. But one adorable little toddler with a purple watering can has undone half of what was done by eleven fifth-graders working all Saturday afternoon.

"It's all my fault!" Hannah cried. "I left the boxes lying on the basement floor! How stupid was that??"

"It's not," I began. "Anyone could have-"

She cut me off. "No!! I should have known better!!!!"

I tried again. "You couldn't have."

"No one will ever forgive me!!" Hannah insisted. "All that work - gone!"

She snapped her fingers. "Like that!! Pouf!!"

I didn't know what to say.

She suddenly brightened. "Maybe we can replace the boxes. You and me, working together."

"We'd have to collect thirty-seven and a half shoe boxes and a ton of wrapping paper," I pointed out. "Then we'd have to wrap them all. That could take weeks."

Hannah sighed deeply. "What are we going to do?"

I thought about it for a few minutes. "Does it really matter if thirty-seven and a half boxes got destroyed?" I finally said.

"Does it really matter?" Hannah repeated incredulously. "I can't believe you asked that."

"Do the math! We still have seventy boxes filled with gifts," I said. "That's about three times as many as we originally planned when Ms. Kantor was here."

"But only two-thirds of what we should have," Hannah retorted.

I shrugged. "I'm not upset about the boxes. Why do you think that everyone else will be?"

"You're my friend," Hannah said, as if that explained everything.

"So? Everyone else likes you, too," I said.

"Maybe," Hannah said doubtfully. "Until they find out."

"Tell them what happened," I urged. "You'll feel better."

"No," Hannah said. "I <u>can't</u>."

Neither of us spoke for a few minutes.

"What will we do with the extra gifts?" I finally asked.

"Can we make them disappear without anyone noticing?" Hannah asked.

Help! Help! Help! Hannah really is a friend in need. I hope I can be a friend, indeed. But she doesn't agree with anything I suggest. What can I do??

"Come in!" Mr. Weston called, without turning around to see who had knocked on the classroom door. It was Thursday afternoon. He was writing math problems on the board for the students to copy for homework.

"I'm from the newspaper." A man with a gray beard entered the room. He carried a camera on a strap around his neck and a notepad in his hand.

Everyone sat up in their chairs.

"The kids are expecting you," Mr. Weston said. He pointed to the pile of gift boxes at the back of the room. "You can see all the work they've put into this project."

Brianna smoothed her hair. "Where's the photographer?"

"That's me," the reporter said.

"They told us they were sending a reporter *and* a photographer," Brianna said.

The reporter winked. "I have a split personality." He took a pen out of his pocket. "Who wants to answer a few questions?"

Brianna waved her hand wildly in the air. "I will!" She jumped to her feet. "I'm the *best* . . ."

"Was it your idea?" the reporter asked her.

"Of course!" Brianna said.

A cry of protest rose from the class. Everyone began to speak at once.

Mr. Weston held up his hand. "One at a time, please."

Mason pointed to Abby. "Ask her!! She organized most of it!!"

Abby shrugged. "Hannah and I were partners." She told the reporter how the idea had been Ms. Kantor's. Then she explained that extra gifts had come in so they had spent all Saturday afternoon decorating more shoe boxes.

The reporter made rapid notes on his paper. "It sounds like a group effort."

"It's for our teacher, Ms. Kantor," Natalie said. "She's away taking care of her sick mother. We want her to be proud of us."

"And it's for kids who don't get any gifts at the holidays," Abby added.

"Show me a box," the reporter said.

"We have most of them here," Hannah explained. "Others are still at my house." She glanced quickly at Abby.

Hannah had made excuses for several days about why she hadn't brought all the boxes to school. No one had caught on yet.

"This is very impressive," the reporter said as he saw the piles of boxes. "You're going to make a lot of kids happy over the holidays." He unscrewed the cover from the lens and looked through the viewfinder of the camera.

The reporter gestured to Abby and Hannah. "You two! Organizers! I want a picture of you together!"

The two girls stood in front of the wrapped gifts and put their arms around each other's shoulders.

"Smile!" the reporter said. He clicked the camera three times. "Perfect! Now for a group shot of the class."

Brianna pushed in front of Bethany. "*I* arranged this newspaper article, you know."

"And we're all *soooo* grateful," Natalie retorted. "Especially since you spent so much time wrapping boxes with us."

"Where *is* my pink box?" Brianna demanded in a huff. "When are you bringing it in, Hannah? You promised it yesterday."

Hannah's smile faded. "I — " she began. "I — "

"*Well?*" Brianna said. She smiled brightly at the camera.

The shutter clicked. The reporter screwed on the lens cap. "That's it, kids," he said.

"*What?* No picture of *me* alone?" Brianna cried furiously.

" 'Fraid not," the reporter said, stuffing his notebook in his coat pocket. "Thanks, everyone! The article will be in the features section of next Wednesday's paper."

As soon as he had left, Brianna turned to Hannah. "You and Abby hogged all the attention," she snapped. "You *purposely* left my box at your house! And all the others, too!"

"That's not true," Hannah began. She looked as if she were about to cry.

"I want my box *now*." Brianna's cheeks were bright red. "I'm coming over to your house after school to get it."

Everyone looked at Hannah. She didn't say a word.

"You can't have your box," Abby heard herself saying.

"Why not?" Brianna demanded.

"Because," Abby said loudly, "her baby sister wrecked it."

Chapter 13

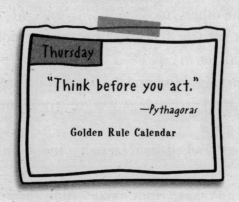

Thursday

"Think before you act."
—Pythagoras

Golden Rule Calendar

Ha!

That's exactly what I <u>didn't</u> do. I acted before I thought. Or rather, I blurted before I thought. The words came out of my mouth before I even knew I was saying them.

Hannah covered her face with her hands. I began to babble an explanation.

"Elena got into the basement, and she saw the watering can. She thought the boxes looked thirsty. Or maybe she thought they were funny-shaped flowers. Or that they were fish. So she watered as many of them as she could."

Then, after blurting all that, I couldn't say another word. I looked nervously around me.

What I Expected to See and Hear
Mad classmates yelling furious words at me and Hannah.

What I Actually Saw and Heard
Kind classmates laughing and speaking friendly words.

Actual Comments from Fellow Students
Mason: Hey, it's no big deal! I know a kid who drank his big brother's bowl of goldfish!!!

Bethany: My little sisters dumped grape juice over all my math book last year.

Natalie: When I was two, I flushed my father's glasses down the toilet.

Tyler: In kindergarten, I scribbled on a wall in my living room with permanent marker.

Hannah uncovered her face. She frowned. She laughed. Then she looked like she was going to cry.

"You should have seen what my sister did to those boxes!" Hannah said. "She soaked them! She turned them into a runny, soggy, gooey mess!

"Thirty-seven runny, soggy, gooey messes," she added in a small voice. "And a half."

Mason shrugged. "So? We still have plenty of gifts."

"Without boxes to put them in," Hannah said.

"It wasn't your fault," Bethany said sympathetically. "I know what little sisters are like. I have two of them!"

"The newspaper reporter saw most of the boxes, anyway," Zach said. "So who cares?"

"You're not mad?" Hannah said disbelievingly. "_Really?_"

"Nobody's perfect," Natalie said. "Thank goodness."

Hannah's Reaction
Astonishment, amazement, disbelief, gratitude, happiness, rejoicing, jubilance, ecstatic joy . . .

Only Fellow Student Who Was Not Happy
Brianna clutched her heart and cried dramatically: "My pink box! Ruined!"

Mr. Weston Saves the Day
He suggested that Brianna make a new pink box.

Brianna's Response
"Oh, no, I can't do that! My pink box can never be replaced!"

Mr. Weston's Suggestion
"Shall we give it a funeral?"

Brianna's Response, Part II
Tossed head back and refused to say another word.

One Final Problem
What to do with the extra gifts (of course).

Hannah and I asked the class what they thought.

Our Classmates' Solutions

1. Bethany: Instead of gift boxes, use gift bags. We can all bring in brown paper bags, fill them, and tie them up with ribbons.

(Note: This is a great idea and much easier to do than decorating shoe boxes!)

2. Mason: Divide all the extra toys into three or four large boxes and donate them to after-school programs.

(Note: Another easy, good idea!)

3. Natalie: What about the police department gift drive?

(*Note: Easiest of all. But, hey, I thought Natalie hated this idea!*)

4. Zach, Brianna, Jonathan: *Named several holiday gift drives, and suggested making donations to all of them.*

Solutions to Our Solutions

1. We are taking a class vote. We will decide together which solution to pick. Mr. Weston said it will be an exercise in democracy.

2. If there is a tie, Hannah and I will cast the deciding vote.

I am voting for number three, the police department gift drive, since it's the easiest, quickest solution.

Hannah is voting for number one, the gift bag idea. That will be easy, too.

And the Winner Is

Solution number four!!!!
(Brianna is <u>already</u> bragging. <u>She's</u> one of the people who proposed it!)

What Happened Next

1. We divided the extra gifts into groups.
2. We labeled each group of gifts with the name of a gift drive.
3. At the end of the school day, we 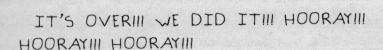 loaded everything into Ms. Yang's car. She will deliver the gifts on behalf of our class this weekend.

IT'S OVER!!! WE DID IT!!! HOORAY!!! HOORAY!!! HOORAY!!!

Chapter 14

Wednesday

"Can we ever have **too much** of a good thing?"

—Cervantes

Extension Cord Calendar

Answer: NO

<u>Good Things We Can't Have Too Much Of</u>

1. Gifts for underprivileged kids.
2. Friends who help out when you're in trouble.
3. Kind words when disaster strikes.
4. Ideas.

<u>Another Good Thing We Can't Have Too Much Of</u>

A newspaper article about the gift box project, with a picture of Hannah and me at the top of the page. <u>In color!!</u>

My family bought ten copies of the newspaper. Hannah's family got fourteen!

"Did you see this?" Casey asked as he hurried to meet Hannah and Abby on the playground that morning. He was holding a copy of the newspaper. "You're famous!!"

Pretending to be embarrassed, Abby hid her face behind her hands. "Nooooooo!"

Hannah laughed. "My dad said we got our fifteen minutes of fame."

"It's, like, only a *local* newspaper, you know," Victoria said scornfully. "What are you, like, getting so excited about?"

"My name is on thousands of theater programs all the time," Brianna announced.

"Did you read what Mr. Weston said about us?" Natalie interrupted. She pointed to the article and began to read. " 'Substitutes are always nervous about going into a new class, but this was one terrific bunch of kids!' "

Natalie continued. "Listen to what else he said: 'Even though their teacher was gone, they organized and completed a charitable project on their own. They even expanded its scope.' "

" 'Expanded its scope,' " Hannah repeated. "That has a nice ring to it."

"Mr. Weston is the greatest!" Natalie said.

"We should do something nice for him," Bethany suggested.

"An apple for the teacher," Abby said. "Only one this time," she added hurriedly as the other kids began to laugh.

"Let's *not* give Mr. Weston an apple," Zach said.

"Apples," Brianna said with a shudder. "I will never touch another apple in my life."

"Like, you won't eat *apples*? Like, why not?" Victoria demanded.

For once, Brianna was at a loss for words. She opened her mouth and then shut it.

"Like, because," Natalie said. "Like, you know."

"I'm glad I'm not in Ms. Kantor's class," Victoria sneered. "You're all, like, so babyish."

"They're not babyish!" Casey sprang to everyone's defense. "My mother was really impressed when she read the article this morning!"

"Like, my mother didn't bother," Victoria snapped.

"Can she read?" Casey asked.

Victoria's eyes narrowed. But before she could reply, Ms. Yang approached the group of fifth-graders.

"Congratulations, everyone," Ms. Yang said. "That's a super article. I'll put it up on the front hall bulletin board with the pictures of your gift boxes. Maybe you'll inspire other classes to do charitable projects of their own."

"All right!" Zach said.

"Is Mr. Weston going to be our substitute until Ms. Kantor gets back?" Hannah asked the principal. "Please say yes!"

"Can Ms. Bunder teach creative writing again?" Abby asked.

Ms. Yang didn't answer. "It's time to go to your classroom," she said, checking her watch. She hurried away.

"Maybe we should get that newspaper reporter to come back to write a second article," Abby said as she walked up the stairs with Hannah and her other friends.

"About Elena watering the boxes?" Hannah suggested.

"I can see the headlines now," Abby said. "Baby Makes a Splash with Holiday Gift Boxes."

Mr. Weston wasn't inside the classroom. There wasn't a teacher in sight.

"Who will we have today?" asked Hannah.

"It won't be Ms. Lee again, will it?" Abby said nervously.

"If it is, I'm organizing a protest at City Hall!" Brianna announced.

"Let's start an Elena Avalanche," Mason said. "I'll teach her to burp."

"Yeah, let's," Zach began, then suddenly stopped.

A familiar figure stood at the door, smiling at the students.

"Ms. Kantor is back!!!" Abby cried. "Ms. Kantor!!!"

Chapter 15

Thursday

"Health is wealth."

Daily Doctor Calendar

If this is true, Ms. Kantor's mother is very wealthy. She has her health back. She doesn't need Ms. Kantor to take care of her anymore.

Now Ms. Kantor can be our teacher again.

Three cheers for Ms. Kantor!!! Hooray! Hooray! Hooray!

Ms. Kantor is happy to be back in class with us. She said she missed us all. (I wonder if she missed Brianna's bragging and Mason's burping.)

We showed Ms. Kantor the newspaper article. She was amazed!!!!! She had tears in her eyes when she heard how the entire school had donated gifts and how we had made extra boxes. "You _are_ a terrific bunch of kids," she said.

She said she was especially proud of me and Hannah for _our_ leadership of the class.

(Does that mean that Ms. Kantor thinks that _I'm_ a leader?)

We also told Ms. Kantor what Elena had done. She had tears in her eyes again, but this time they were from laughing.

We told her about Ms. Lee (but not about the Apple Avalanche) and about Mr. Weston.

"You had an exciting time while I was gone," Ms. Kantor commented. "Maybe you can all write stories about it for creative writing."

Ms. Bunder is coming back tomorrow!!!

The word "hooray!" is not enough. Is there a super hooray? Or a mega hooray?

Or an ultra hooray? (Why do they all sound like dish detergents?)

HOORAY!!!!
That's better.

HOORAY!!!!

That's even better.

HOORAY!!!

Ms. Yang just came into our classroom. She said that she distributed our gifts over the weekend. Some of the kids who received boxes asked if they could write to us!!!!

Ms. Yang gave them the address of the school. "You'll be getting letters soon," she said. "Maybe you'll make new friends or get a pen pal."

"Awesome," Mason said.

"This is better than a newspaper article," Natalie said.

"No way!" Brianna said, tossing her hair over her shoulder.

"We can tell the kids about how Elena watered the boxes," suggested Hannah. "Do you think they'd like to hear about that?"

"Certainly," Ms. Yang said. She waved to us and left the classroom.

I raised my hand. "I bet some of the kids have little brothers or sisters, too."

"Or pets?" Bethany said hopefully.

"You'll discover lots of things about one another," Ms. Kantor said. She picked up a piece of chalk and went to the blackboard. "It's time for math."

AWWWWW!!!

I was hoping Ms. Kantor would forget about math! Or at least give us a break for a day or two.

I guess things really are back to normal now.